A Character Building Book™

Learning About Resilience From the Life of
Lance Armstrong

Brenn Jones

The Rosen Publishing Group's
PowerKids Press™
New York

To George and Michelle

Published in 2002 by The Rosen Publishing Group, Inc.
29 East 21st Street, New York, NY 10010

First Edition

Book Design: Michael Caroleo

Project Editor: Emily Raabe

Photo Credits: pp. 4, 15 © Reuters NewMedia Inc./CORBIS; p. 7 © Reuters/Jacky Naegelen/Archive Photos; p. 8 © Reuters/Robert Pratta/Archive Photos; pp. 11, 12 © Associated Press AP; p. 16 © Reuters/Eric Gaillard/Archive Photos; p. 19 © AFP/CORBIS; p. 20 © Reuters/Jean-Paul Pelissier/Archive Photos.

Jones, Brenn.
    Learning about resilience from the life of Lance Armstrong / Brenn Jones.
      p. cm.— (A character building book)
    Includes index.
    Summary: This is a brief biography of Lance Armstrong, resilient cancer survivor who returned to his bike racing and who won the 1999 and the 2000 Tour de France.
    ISBN 0-8239-5779-9
    1. Armstrong, Lance—Juvenile literature. 2. Cyclists—United States—Biography—Juvenile literature. 3.Cancer—Patients—United States—Biography—Juvenile literature. [1. Armstrong, Lance. 2. Bicyclists. 3. Cancer—Patients.] I. Title. II. Series.
    GV1051.A76 J66 2002   00-012002
    796.6'2'092—dc21
    [B]

Manufactured in the United States of America

Contents

1   Resilience   5

2   Like Mother, Like Son   6

3   Early Success   9

4   Cancer   10

5   Chemotherapy   13

6   Recovery   14

7   Back on the Bike   17

8   Tour de France   18

9   Riding to Victory   21

10 Lance Armstrong Foundation   22

    Glossary   23

    Index   24

    Web Sites   24

Resilience

Some things in life are difficult. The ability to succeed when things are hard is called resilience. Lance Armstrong is a bike racer who has a lot of resilience. In 1996, Lance got cancer. Many people thought Lance would never race again. Over the next few years Lance went through a difficult time of treatment and recovery from the disease. In 1999, Lance showed his incredible resilience by winning the Tour de France, the most challenging bicycle race in the world. In 2000, Lance did it again!

◀ *This is Lance (center) biking in the 1999 Tour de France.*

Like Mother, Like Son

Lance Armstrong was born on September 18, 1971. He grew up in Plano, Texas. When he was growing up, Lance did not know his father, but he was very close to his mother. She worked hard to take care of him. Lance learned to be resilient like her.

When he was in high school, Lance was hit by a car while he was riding his bike. The doctor told him to rest for three weeks. Lance wanted to compete in a race so badly that he didn't listen to the doctor. One week later Lance came in third in a **triathlon**.

This is Lance's mom, kissing him after a victory in a 1999 race in France. Lance named his house in Austin, Texas, "Casa Linda" after his mother. ▶

Early Success

By the time Lance finished high school in 1990, he was good enough at bicycling to race in Europe. Lance raced for the United States at the 1992 Summer Olympics in Barcelona, Spain. He finished 14th in the road race there. In 1993, when he was 21 years old, Lance won the World Championships. King Harold of Norway wanted to congratulate Lance on his victory. Lance made sure that his mother met the king, too.

Lance kept getting better after the World Championships, and he kept winning races.

◀ *In 1993, Lance was the youngest rider ever to win one of the daily races, or stages, of the Tour de France. He was only 21 years old.*

Cancer

In 1996, Lance won a race in North Carolina called the Tour DuPont. Usually Lance felt good after a race, especially when he won. At the end of the Tour DuPont, though, he felt tired and sick. Lance felt worse and worse until, finally, he was too sick to ride his bike. Lance went to a doctor to find out what could be happening. The doctor told him some bad news. Lance had cancer. The cancer had spread to his lungs and to his brain. Lance's case was serious. He would have to get very strong treatment.

This is Lance (center) after he won the Tour DuPont in 1996. ▶

Chemotherapy

Lance had surgery to get the cancer out of his brain. He also needed **chemotherapy**. Chemotherapy is hard on the patient. Doctors put **toxins** into the patient's blood to kill the cancer. The toxins kill the cancer, but they also make the patient weak. Lance had to take the strongest form of chemotherapy. During chemotherapy he lost weight and became very sick. Lance wanted to stay active and to keep riding his bike, but chemotherapy made him too weak to get out of bed. Doctors did not know if Lance would survive the treatment.

◀ *Even though he was sick, Lance kept a positive attitude and was able to make jokes. He even named his cat Chemo, for his treatment.*

Recovery

Lance was in chemotherapy for three months. After the three months, he still had to get treatments that left him feeling weak. Lance began to recover, but it was difficult for him to get back into racing. He had lost a lot of weight and strength.

After the treatments, Lance gave himself some time to relax and to recover. He decided to slow down for a little while. He also fell in love with a woman named Kristin Richard. Lance and Kristin traveled together through Europe while Lance got better.

This is Lance giving a speech in New York City. The woman next to him is Kristin. Lance and Kristin got married in 1998. ▶

Back on the Bike

Lance's friends believed that Lance could ride again. They encouraged him to get back in shape. In April 1998, Lance decided to train hard for a week to see how he felt. He went to North Carolina, where he had won the Tour DuPont twice. He rode his bike up the hills and through the forests. Lance remembered how much he loved bicycling. He also realized that he was strong enough to ride fast again. Lance soon had a new goal. He wanted to win the 1999 Tour de France!

◀ *This is Lance in 1998, at a morning training session for the men's road World Cycling Championship.*

Tour de France

The first Tour de France was held in 1903. Sixty bicyclists entered the race but only 21 were able to finish it. The Tour de France lasts over three weeks. Bicyclists race over 2,200 miles (3,520 km) of France's cities, countryside, and mountains. Each day is its own race, called a stage. At the end of the Tour de France, whichever rider has the fastest time overall wins.

Today, more than 200 bicyclists from around the world enter the Tour de France. Many don't finish it. Lance wanted to win it.

This is Lance at the beginning of one of the stages of the 1999 Tour de France. ▶

Riding to Victory

Lance and his team, the U.S. Postal Service, entered the 1999 Tour de France. Lance won the first stage. Since he was winning, Lance got to wear the leader's yellow jersey. Members of Lance's team rode in front of him to block the wind. Lance rode behind them. This is called **drafting**. At the end of each stage Lance would burst ahead. Lance won three more stages in the race. After increasing his lead in the mountains, Lance rode into Paris on June 25, winning the 1999 Tour de France.

Lance was the first American to win the Tour de France since Greg LeMond in 1990. Everyone was amazed to hear about the cancer survivor who was resilient enough to win the world's most difficult bicycle race.

Lance Armstrong Foundation

In 2000, Lance and the U.S. Postal Service Team again entered the Tour de France. It didn't seem possible that Lance could win again. Guess what? He did it. Lance won the 2000 Tour de France, as well!

What will Lance do next? He will keep racing. Lance also will work to help cancer patients. He has started a **foundation** that works to help find a cure for cancer and to educate people about the disease. Lance's hard work has paid off. His resilience is a message to the world about what cancer survivors can do.

Glossary

chemotherapy (KEE-moh-ther-uh-pee) Medicine that fights cancer.

drafting (DRAFT-ing) Following closely behind another person in a bike race.

foundation (fown-DAY-shun) An organization that is set up to give money to support a cause, and to educate people about that cause.

toxins (TOK-sins) Poisons.

triathlon (try-ATH-lon) A race that is made up of swimming, bicycling, and running.

Index

C
chemotherapy, 13,
    14

E
Europe, 9, 14

N
North Carolina,
    10, 17

O
Olympics, 9

P
Plano, Texas, 6

R
Richard, Kristin, 14

T
Tour de France, 5,
    17, 18, 21, 22

Tour DuPont, 10,
    17

U
U.S. Postal Service,
    21, 22

W
World
    Championships,
    9

Web Sites

To learn more about Lance Armstrong and resilience, check out these Web sites:
http://www.lancearmstrong.com
http://www.laf.org